Radio Water

flash fiction by
Francine Witte

Roadside Press

RADIO WATER
Copyright © Francine Witte, 2024
ISBN: 979-8-8690-5532-3

Editor: Michele McDannold

Roadside Press
Meredosia, Illinois

Table of Contents

Night is a Man

A man without hands, without feet. Night has nothing but eyes and ears and a scrap of heart.

You left ten weeks ago, and Night is what I sleep with.

Tonight, I wake Night up and take him to the grocery store. On the way there, Night looks at the moon, down to a sliver now, but still. If Night had a voice, he would tell me how the moon is his.

I walk up to the doors that whoosh open. Night doesn't fit. He is sky, after all. He is dreams, after all.

I tell Night to wait, and thank God for his ears.

I walk inside, my slippers back home, and I pad my feet down the aisles towards the bags and bags of chips. Since you left me, I look at food. It looks at me. I have put on the weight I was afraid to. If you still loved me, you wouldn't now.

I pay for the chips and slip them into my jacket. They make a bump. They are the child we will never have.

I walk through the doors. The sun has shown up and pushed the darkness aside. I look everywhere, but Night has vanished. All eyes and ears of him. And like you, nothing but a scrap of his heart left behind.

Fishsweat

All over the counter in our bungalow kitchen. My mother, bandanna tying up her tired hair. My mother, asking me how bad I want to eat. *These fish are a mess*, she says, *all slime and goo and fishsweat*. No such thing as fishsweat, I think, but my mother has never, not once in her life, called a thing what it really is.

Every so often she stops to stare out of the gingham window to see if my father's car is pulling up. He said he was going back to that fishing shack we stopped at last night to pick up some bait. Where he asked the young woman who ran it, what was the best spot to fish on the lake. How we all of us heard her saying how she's running the shack by herself since her husband died, her tan belly showing out from her midriff top.

And then my father going out by himself early this morning, coming back with five whole fish, each one slimier and smellier than the one before it, and me having exactly no appetite. Not after watching the sweat trickle out of my mother's bandanna, her wiping it off with the back of her rubber-gloved hand, her thwacking the heads off the fish one by one and tossing them into a bucket like they were somebody's father, somebody's husband. And me standing there next to her, wondering exactly how many fish this is going to take.

How to Answer a Door

Slowly – As if the other side of your life is on the other side of the door. Like the door is an "and" or a "but." You were living a quiet life, AND you opened the door, and your ex was standing there, flowers in hand. This was miles before he was your ex. This was your first date and you saw his ocean eyes and you knew you could drown in them BUT you couldn't help it.

Quickly – As if you have better things to do. Which you do. Or don't. Who can keep up with you anymore? Your ex left you with three squalling – no, adorable kids and no way to feed them. At first, your ex showed up for circus weekends and clown weekends. You took Calgon baths – the bubbles, the phone left ringing in the other room. But then, the ex remarried. The ex became ex-er. New family, et cet. So when the doorbell rings, it's a kid selling hospital candy or Sam from next door who wants to borrow the leaf blower. You answer the door quick between Kid One's Lego tantrum and Kid Two's cereal mess. You worry that if you don't answer, the knocking will never stop.

Asking – Like your mother told you. Always ask, who's there? Who's there? And then? You said. Well, you open the door, she said. No, no you meant, what if it's a bad person? Like a man who says he will love you and doesn't? You should be glad a man will want you in the first place, your mother means but doesn't say. Instead, she says you worry too much about everything and it's going to give you wrinkles.

Not asking – You don't really have to. You will know if it's an emergency. There will be sirens, there will be pounding. If it's only important, but not emergency it will continue. It will be like a man who tells you he loves you, let's get married and he's not asking again. He will tell you to remember the time he took you to the ocean and you said that the water was too salty, too fishy and that he had to convince you to stick in a toe and how you finally liked it. He will tell you should listen to your mother and stop worrying about everything. He will tell you to forget that the ocean can drown you. It doesn't do that every time.

Waiting – This is the best way to answer the door. Wait until the knocking stops. It could take years, but it will. Wait until it all dies down – the tapping, the rapping, the scraping, the swishing, the cooing, the ocean eyes, the words of love, the fear that no one will even knock again.

In Another Language, Your Name Means Murder

But did I listen? No.

Not when the old women drew pictures of knives and mimicked throatsqueeze. Not when danger music played in the background *ba-ba-bom*. Not even when subtitles – *run for your life!* – zippered across your chest.

I looked instead at the cool blue ice of your eyes. I told myself a lot gets lost in translation, and murder probably means something else, a shade of difference. I told myself that murder is relative and that the dagger you were holding was to carve our names in a tree heart. I told myself that a warning is nothing anyway, just a lost ship on a murky sea, turning and turning, seagulls screaming in the air above, no hope of finding land.

Mimi Comes to the Door and No One Can Stop Her

"Dad home?" she says, looking past my shoulder like I'm going to lie to her. Mimi is one of those big, blowsy blondes you never think you're going to meet in real life.

"He's out back," I tell her. "Garden Day, y'know?" Saturday morning and Dad wearing his Hawaiian shirt and straw hat. Likes to get his hands in the dirt, he says.

Mimi's red lipstick is clown-mouth creepy, and she has blue eyeshadow at 10 a.m. It's weird, but my dad finds her sexy. An interesting woman, he told us over supper after she first moved next door. I held my food in my mouth, not even a chew. I knew what interesting meant.

"How about your Ma?" Mimi says. "That's who I really want to talk to."

Shit, I think. She's finally going to do it. Mimi's had three husbands, and now she wants my dad to be her fourth.

It's the first day of summer vacation, and I was looking forward to hanging out some at Jennifer's pool. It's only an above-ground, no diving or anything, and we all know her little brother pees in it, but still.

"You tell your mother yet?" Mimi looks at me, the top of her beehive ruffling a bit. At first, I think she's talking about her and my father, and then I realize what she means.

"Oh that," I say. "I was waiting to see if I get my period."

"It's okay," she says. "If you have a kid and your Ma don't want you, you can live with your dad and me."

It had happened so fast, me telling Mimi. I was sitting on the porch last week, and she drove up in her little Barbie convertible. She had shopping bags from *Lindy's*, a tacky downtown store that has lots of nightgowns and garter belts in the window. I was crying because that was the day I usually get my period. I'm so regular, so lunar, Jennifer says, that the minute I missed, we knew.

Mimi sat down next to me. "People like sex," she said, "it's okay." I don't know, I could have lied. I really could. I could have said something like I failed trig, which I did, or that I'm scared I wouldn't have much to do this summer, which I don't.

Somehow though, when Mimi looked at me, I didn't notice her eyeshadow, her botchy lipstick. I just saw someone who really listened to me. No one does that anymore.

But now, with Mimi standing there ready to swoop my dad away, I knew I had to stop her. Mimi was good to talk to and all, but she isn't anyone's mother.

So when Mimi asks again if my mother is home, I look her straight in her face. "No," I lie. "Shopping Day," I lie again.

My mother is, in fact, in the next room. Water blasting over the breakfast plates and how does Mimi not hear that?

"I'll come back later," Mimi says. "It's time your mother knew. Your dad isn't happy with her." Then, she lowers her voice to a whisper. "And listen, you're 16 but you're old enough to know about boys, about men. How in the end they never do you right."

I think about my dad. How aside from getting involved with Mimi, he's a pretty square guy. Drives me to dances, gives me ten bucks whenever I ask. And maybe I do get the Mimi thing. Her other three husbands liked her, too. But I don't want my dad to end up in one of her warnings about men some day.

I tell Mimi, I'm okay. How I know about boys, and I'm sure my thing will work out because I'm starting to feel a little crampy, and there I go lying again.

"I'll be back later," Mimi says, and walks across our lawn back to her house, the heels of her leopard pumps sinking into the grass.

I hear my mother turning off the water. In a minute she will come out and have no idea how she was spared. For now. She will come in, wipe her hands on her apron and smooth my hair and think I'm still a little girl. She will warn me to wear sunscreen if I go to Jennifer's pool even though I've told her how many times that I'm allergic.

In a couple of hours, my dad will come in, and we will all have lunch. He will still be wearing his garden clothes. He will dig dirt out of his fingernails. Good dirt, he will wink when he catches me watching him. I will look at his face, maybe the last time before Mimi comes back and flips our lives over like topsoil.

I will sit there and watch my mother as she makes peanut butter sandwiches, corn chips on the side. "You need protein and carbs to swim and garden," she will smile at me and my dad. I will sit there, trying to will the slightest cramp into my stomach, and think how any minute, Mimi will knock again at the door. I will wish there was some way to stop this. Some magical way to turn us all into one of those tableau things we have to look at in art class. My mother frozen with the knife as she scrapes the inside of a peanut butter jar, my father wiping his hands on his Hawaiian shirt, and me, my mouth hanging open, as if too heavy with secrets about to spill out.

Rumble

On the bus to her mother's funeral, and Maizie forgot to bring money. No point to turn back now. Already Ohio. Maizie has no credit and no friends to text for cash.

Her mother, turns out, died from alcohol poisoning. No surprise. Stepfather Dave called with the news, said he'd pay for the bus ticket and all she had to do was pick it up. Said he'd be waiting for her at the station.

Maizie only met Stepfather Dave the one time. She was 18 and succulent. He offered her a Coke and Maizie could swear he slipped something in it. She told him she wasn't thirsty.

The bus is rolling through Ohio and it all seems postcard now. Ten years the hell away from here, and it's been nothing but server jobs, a beaty boyfriend or two, and yeah, succulent isn't her anymore.

The man sitting next to her is sweaty and suited and eating a sandwich. Ham with lettuce from the looks of it. Toasty and warm from the smell of it. He picked it up at the rest stop ten miles back. The hole in Maizie's stomach widening like the Ohio countryside. Maizie's wallet back home on her nightstand, plump with her last 200 bucks and Jack, the guy she left in her apartment, will find the cash and use it to drink a hole into the universe.

An hour later, the bus pulls into the last stop, her stop. The screech of brakes. The bus lowering into a hiss. The driver gets out and starts pulling suitcases out of the bus belly.

Stepfather Dave is waiting. Leaned up against the dead river green of his station wagon. He is scanning the people getting off the bus, one by one. His face goes off like a light bulb about to blow when he sees Maizie, waves her over.

She gets in the car. The suitcase in front of her scrunching up her legs. Stepfather Dave says, "you look good. The city pudged you up a touch, but I like it." The tiny rumble of her stomach, the engine starting up.

He offers her a Coke, this time with the cap still on. She takes it and unscrews it. He digs in his pocket and says, "all's I got is this chocolate bar." His eyes go from the road to her thighs and back again. Outside, the pure empty of everything around them, in front of them, and when he unwraps the candy bar with a single expert motion, she takes it.

Dad Always Looked Like a Mountain

Or a billy goat climbing the mountain, or a group of climbers at the top of the mountain. All of it huge and not speaking to us.

Mom shrugged and made breakfast. She would ask the mountain if it wanted coffee even though it never answered her, of course. How could it? Mountains have no mouths, billy goats have no words, and the climbers can't waste their thin-air breath on my silly hopeful mother.

My brothers and I were used to it all. Dad on the evening couch, sports humming the TV, evening newspapers moving up and down across his snoozy chest. Later, we knew the billy goat part of Dad would eat the newspapers, but not before the climber part checked the paper to see if there was a story about them.

One night, though, Dad didn't come home. We all pretended to be sad, but we knew it was a party. Mom stringing the walls with crepe paper, relieved that Dad wouldn't eat it. Happy that she could stop asking a silent mountain if it wants coffee every damn day. Happy to block out the climbers' constant chatter and high-fiving.

Only my brother, sitting in the corner, seemed sad for real, his almost-hoof growing inside his converse sneaker, though we didn't see it, his face going sullen and rockcraggy, his fingers quietly climbing his chest.

Dirt

The man on the TV is selling soap. Says it will clean anything. The woman looks at her husband, who is snoring up the evening. Snoring up her life. She puts it on her list.

At the supermarket, she asks the clerk about the TV soap. He looks the woman up and down and motions her to follow him to the back.

The doors swing closed behind us as he points to a purple curtain. "You sure about this?" he says.

"The man on the TV said this will clean anything. My husband's clothes," the woman says.

"I understand," the clerk pulls back the curtain. "I can see you're quite unhappy," the clerk says, his head tilted to the side. With this, the woman bursts into tears.

Later that night, the woman mixes the cleaner into a bucket of water. "Be careful not to touch it with your bare hands," the clerk had warned. She looks around. The lemony bubbles stinging her nose. The cleanness that is about to happen.

Next morning, the clerk shows up. Dressed in a Sunday suit, and holding a bouquet of daisies.

The woman lets him in. She looks young and new somehow. "A miracle," she says, offering the clerk a seat on the couch. "It lifted stains from the carpet that hadn't budged for years."

"Yes," said the clerk. "It's very effective." He looks over

at the chair where he guesses the husband might have sat. "It vanishes every bit of dirt it touches." He straightens his tie and pulls the woman next to him on the couch. "That's why we say to wear gloves."

Anywhere by the Sea

Grab of waterfingers under your toes and horizon sailboats. This could be anywhere but it's not. It's not your ice cream ocean from when you were nine, and your mother held a towel around you as you wriggled into drier clothes. Not the goodbye sand when Bobby Epstein kissed you one last twilight time, his face lit up by the bonfire collapsing, snapping, and Julie Mitchell's face lit up sudden behind him.

Now, the sea creeps deeper, up around your ankles. Washy and warm for April. Light seeping out of the five o'clock sky. All of it going older and you can't make it stop. This could be anywhere but it isn't. You think how every shore everywhere has to look the same. Combination of boats and sand and half-built castles. Maybe an ice cream stick here and there. Up above, the sky, the same combination of blue and whisper of waiting moon, and you, with the tide reaching high as your knees, collection of cells and eyelashes and memories, same as everyone, anywhere, standing there, feeling the slightest bit of undertow, and knowing how easy the tide could pull you in if you let it.

Cross-country

An hour into our cross-country car ride, I realize I hate
Harry. I look at his sockless feet in the brown leather
loafers. A smug look that stretches all the way up to his
face.

XXX

Near Philly, I tell Harry I need to pee. You always need
to pee, he says. And that's true. Peeing is like smoking for
me. A way to get myself out of the world for two minutes.
I have been holding it in since New York. Harry exhales,
his breath smugging up the air. He turns off at the next
exit. Too late, I tell him. My favorite undies soaked against
the seat.

XXX

Okay, this is out of sequence, but important. It's five days
later. Outside Arizona. I have, by now, murdered Harry.
Stuffed him in the trunk under his duffel. We were going
to hike the Grand Canyon. The duffel is bulging with
hiking gear. Right now, it's holding Harry down like a
paper weight.

XXX

Back to now. Harry is arguing with the GPS. "You'd drive
us into a lake, you nitwit." Good one, Harry, I say. Usually,
I admire his pluck with electronics. How he yells at his
fitness tracker for not counting enough steps. How he
yells at the blender, *stop, it's already a smoothie.* But today,
everything's bothering me about Harry.

XXX

Days later, we stop for lunch in Kansas or Missouri or Kansas. The waitress is young and Harry is looking at her up and down. "Eyes on the menu," I finally say. "Don't you have to pee?" he asks. And I do. Like crazy. Only there's no way I'm leaving the table. I pee right there on the vinyl seat. Harry looks shocked. The waitress looks shocked. I'll have the eggs, I simply say.

XXX

In Colorado, we find one of those stops where truckers take showers. I tell the guy at the counter I'm having woman troubles. He nods and says his mother has that and warns that we don't get many women, so it might be a little rough in there. I tell him I've seen rough. I look at Harry. I'll be fine, I say.

XXX

Back in the car, I notice lipstick on Harry's collar. I wish he wasn't such a cliché. It must have happened while I was in the shower. While I was trying not to notice the girlie pictures slapped all over the walls. Harry must have found something in the hooker aisle and taken it out back. Whatever it was wore blood-red lipstick. I tell Harry we need to find a hardware store.

XXX

We find one somewhere in Utah. I tell Harry if we're hiking, we'll need to build a fire. Good thinking, he says. I walk over to the axe aisle and pick out a small one. I run the blade along his fingers. I run the blade along his neck. "Let's get you some hiking socks," I say. We go up to the counter. He motions to the restroom. "Go now," he says.

"You know how you can get."

XXX

Don't worry, I tell him. I'm good.

The We Part

At first, we didn't know it was a gunshot.

We, being me, as Nathan was actually asleep. Which actually is most of the time.

The street below our apartment is filled with people, even at 2 a.m. Nathan said we shouldn't move in above a bar. I think he also meant we shouldn't move in, but the me part of we won out, saying it was a good commute to work. Somehow, I thought that might help things.

It didn't.

I don't think we've had one good night together since we lived here. And the me part of we hasn't slept for ten whole minutes in a row. The Nathan part of we comes home and doses himself with a melatonin/cough syrup combo. Insists it's to block out the noise from the bar.

Another bang or boom or whatever. Most nights, the me part of we tries to not hear the breaking glass, the fuck-you, man's, the throat clear of the constant Harleys. Most nights I sit up watching Nathan. He is REM-sleeping, his eyelids all jumpy, maybe the only part of him that moves anymore when I'm around. Don't you hear all that noise, Nathan? the me part of we is asking. I pretend he is stroking my hair, "shhh, I love you," he is saying.

The me part of we wonders what to do about the noise outside. What's the best thing to do with a gunshot? Do you run towards it or away? The me part of we wonders the same thing about love.

Nathan is lying there, snoring up the night like a chainsaw, like a motorcycle, like a man who is ignoring me. All of those things more danger than a gun.

I look out the window to the street below. Light swirl of cop cars and a shot man on the ground. Woman in handcuffs, "I love you, I love you," she says as they lead her away. Love kills again. I look back at Nathan. Drifting and distant and not any part of we anymore.

Quiet now. Quiet enough to close my eyes. The only sound is Nathan snoring, the buzz of it cutting a hole just big enough for me to crawl out of.

Lady Macbeth at the Nail Salon

She tells you not to stare at the blood. You say that her hand is clean, a bit too clean, in fact, all papery and raw. You tell her she doesn't have to soak her fingers, but she insists. Says she likes the way the bubbles tickle her nostrils, that the lemon scent soothes her down. You ask her why she's so jittery, her fingers shaking like twigs. She asks if you are married. "If you were," she says, "you'd understand." She looks around the nail salon, the ferns spilling out of their baskets, the hum of drying fans. "You like all this?" she asks you. "Doing manicures all day?" She tilts her head toward the salon owner, squatty and cat-eyed, sprawled out in a pedicure chair. She is eating a salad like you don't have time for. "Wouldn't you rather do that?" Lady Macbeth asks, and you realize how happy you have been all this time not being happy. You think about your husband, his late nights working and so little to show. The lemon starts to tickle your nostrils. You take Lady Macbeth's hand, your fingers entwined. What felt like twigs feels steely now and strong. She pulls her hand from yours and hands you a nail file. She looks at you and then at the owner. "Yes," you think, "yes." You think how nice it would be to tell your husband he could quit his job at night and keep you company. You wonder why it's taken till now for you to realize this, and is it possible you've been sleeping all this time?

There's a Bear in the Window

I swear that's what Murphy just told me. Big, old bear face shining like a dinner plate. All I got to do is turn around and look. That Murphy. He's always saying stuff like that. Bear at the window, bug in the bread, he wants a divorce...

I slip away from the table and go in to pack him up. Tomorrow he's going back out on the road. Big, old truck driver, him. That's okay. With Murphy gone, I get to relax. With Murphy gone, I get to watch TV or just make fudge.

There's a bear at the window, Murphy is still insisting from the kitchen. Maybe *you* can ignore a bear, but *I* can't.

I've never actually made fudge before. I'll probably need a pan.

I finish packing. I even throw in a few forever things for Murphy, next month's calendar, extra towel. Just to humor him about the divorce thing.

Sound of glass breaking. Sound of Murphy's sudden yelp.

I remember the first time Murphy left. Stayed out for two whole months. Then he admitted he couldn't even find his keys without me.

I walk into the kitchen. Walk by Murphy's bloody corpse. I need a perfectly square pan for fudge. I need to grease it. Then I'll need a bowl.

Bear's gone now. Must have just taken that big, old dirt road out of here.

Murphy sure seems dead. Blood all over and eyes fixed straight up at the ceiling.

If Murphy hadn't come back that other time, I'd *swear* he was gone for good.

Mandy Wants to Touch the Horizon

"It's there. I can see it," she says.

She is all floaty wings and bathing cap as she stands on the shoreline. The salty lip of the surf at her feet.

Right nearby, Harry looks happy. Sprawled out on the stripey lounge chair, magazine open on his lap.

"It doesn't exist," he reminds her. The cubes in his iced tea clinking as they melt. They have had this discussion before. Maybe not about the horizon. Maybe it was more about the perfect marriage. He continues thumbing through his magazine, *50 Most Beautiful* issue.

"There's a sailboat sitting right on it," she insists. "And look how the sea meets the sky."

"The horizon is just an illusion," Harry says. He is fixed now on a *moviestarmillionairemogul*. "You think you can touch it, but it only moves farther away."

"Like happiness," she says. She remembers the dead anniversaries. The broiled chickens drowning in the pan.

Harry is almost listening. Lost now on page 24, Miss Montana. Something about the mermaid swirl of her hair, the faraway look in her eyes.

A group of children pat wet sand into a plastic pail. Their giggles sailing into the air like missed opportunities.

Mandy puts her toe in the ocean. She slathers on a coat of sunscreen and inhales as hard as she can. If she leaves now, she can reach the horizon by sundown. Before darkness takes over and blends it all into one thing.

This isn't Anything

When Burley comes home late every night, I tell myself he's busy. He tells me that, too, but I believe it more when I say it.

Now, I do understand. He's been busy before, but this is a busy with a smell on it.

This particular night, it's 9 p.m. exactly. He comes in all fed even though I made pot roast. The pot roast that burned while I waited for him, the flat char of it still coating the air. Burley whooshes himself into the shower. Careful to take off his jeans and shirt and ball them into a wad. "Best to leave those," he says. "I stopped for gas, and some jerk spilled coffee all over me."

I wait till the shower is running to give his shirt a good sniff. Not a hint of coffee anywhere. Nothing is wet. And then I go for his jeans – in the pocket, a matchbook. Red with the black outline of two lovers, two cocktail glasses about to clink.

After the shower and him toweling himself off. "Whatta day" and "I shoulda called."

I hold up the matchbook. "Oh this," he says. "This isn't anything. Guy at work was passing them out. New place opened up down the street."

Burley says, work's gonna be a bear this week, just so I know. He likes to compare everything to animals. Guys at work are a bunch of donkeys. Me, I'm a cute little cat.

And I am. Curled up and patient, like my mother taught me to be. This is what men like, she said. And really, I didn't mind. Although Burley forgets sometimes that a cat needs attention.

A tickle on the back of its neck. A rake of fingers through the hair. Later, in bed, I nuzzle up, kitten-like. He turns on his side. "Tired," is all he says.

I whisper, "hey I'd love to go to that matchbook place with you. Have drinks like we used to." I say this as his breath becomes even with sleep. I wobble his shoulder, and say it again, but he doesn't move. He is a lost mountain to me now.

Something that isn't hunger exactly gets me up on my feet and into the fridge. I pull out the leftover pot roast, burnt as it is. I kitten my face into it. Nuzzle and nibble and suck. Soon I go from tame little cat to feral. I crouch down to the floor and start gnawing like a lion on one of the nature shows I watch when Burley isn't home. And then, without a sound, Burley just like that in the doorway. The swell of the fluorescent light overhead, sudden and sharp.

Burley leans over and struggles the pot roast away from my mouth. A look on his face like he caught me kissing another man. He lifts me to my feet. He flinches as my fingernails dig into his shoulders. Any harder and there would be blood. "What's wrong with you?" he says with a look on his face like one of those animal trainers who realize they've gone too far. "I told you," he says, "none of this is anything." He grabs a dishtowel, wipes the grease off my chin and kisses me down to the floor.

Next morning, the mess from last night all over the kitchen and Burley humming from the bathroom. The pot roast, the dishtowel, the spot on the floor with naked us rubbed into it. I think about asking Burley now to tell me about the gas station. *What was the feel of it,* I want to say. *Who was this guy? Was he bigger than you? Was the coffee hot? Why weren't you burned?*

I clean everything up and put on a pot of coffee, the smell of it filling the room. The same smell that wasn't anywhere on Burley's shirt, and when Burley comes in and kisses me on the cheek, pulls back and winks at me, I feel a million questions on my tongue, a lion's growl forming in my throat.

Remoting

You slide behind Jackson's desk. It's after five and everyone gone. You call your husband from Jackson's phone. Don't forget to dial 9. You tell your husband you forgot to defrost and can he pick up a pizza? Jackson's desk is at the far end of the huge open office, sad little cubicle near *Stairway B.* Jackson's desk is piles of folders, staplers, and multi-colored post-it pads. Also, a bobble head baseball player and a framed photo of Jackson's wife. Full body pic of her waterskiing, hair whipped around her face, and you can still see that she's pretty in a way you aren't. Tight and small and brunette. No wonder Jackson loves her.

XXX

You tell your husband that night he shouldn't have ordered anchovies. They are going to keep you awake, you say. He says this is the first he's heard of this and maybe you could have been home making dinner. He doesn't say any more, but keeps remoting the TV when you want to watch a movie. *Evening news. Car commercial. Game show.* What the hell does he want? You decide you've never met a man who knows what he wants. Not really. You decide that tomorrow will be the day.

XXX

You get in early, way before *Accounting,* way before the coffee cart guy, and way way way before Jackson. You sit at his desk, his chair all cushion and swivel and squeak. You flick the bobble head, your fingers tingly. The bobble head wiggles and nods. You open the drawer and pull out a pen, blue, no red. You pull a post-it off the pad. It's blue which would be a nice background to the red of the ink. You write I LOVE YOU. Heart, heart, heart. You stick the note smack across his wife's beautiful photo face. It flickers that his wife doesn't eat pizza, not with a figure like that, not with her waterskiing like that. How much Jackson would like you better, your comfortable pudge, your Wednesday blouse, a little wrinkled. Jackson could relax with a woman like you. You pull a lick of scotch tape off the roll and thumb it across the top of the post-it. To keep it from blowing away. You look around, all the desks still empty, about to be peopled. You head back to your desk way at the other end. Jackson will never suspect it's you who left the note. Rather, he will pry the note off of his wife's photo, stand there for a moment remoting through the women in the office. Who can it be? Who can it be? Him just standing there, going from one to the next to the next. Never ever sure, you decide, who he would even want it to be.

Drunkdaddy

Punches a hole in the cakey window. The hole is the size of a woman's head. My mother's head. Tells the window, good, now you are broken, too. Blames the window for being so gooked up with grime he couldn't see my mother driving the hell out of our lives. *If I'd seen it*, Drunkdaddy says, *I could have stopped it.* He takes off his t-shirt and wraps it around his bloody knuckles. *Suck it up*, Drunkdaddy tells his nakedchest self. He looks around the living room, stained glass lamp and pom-pom pillows. My mother's piano with the photo gallery on the top. Head shot of her like a movie star. Drunkdaddy picks it right up like he's gonna break that, too, but doesn't. Blood drop after blood drop falling on the rug. He puts the photo back and walks over to the liquor cabinet. Walks right by me and my sister who have been standing there the whole time, too scared to just walk over and tell Drunkdaddy we want to take him to the hospital. But another drunk is about to come on and so we stand there, like all those other times, fear caking up our hands, our legs, and all we can do is watch Drunkdaddy swig the brandy down his throat, his neck going ropey with veins as he sucks it all down, and him wiping his mouth clean with the back of his good hand, turning and looking at the wall behind us, and saying "you're next."

Twins, Prediction

Years from now, grown. Twin One will spend her days in a kitchen stirring casseroles. At night, she will ice her husband's back which is sore from breaking concrete blocks all day.

Twin Two, the happier one, will be a *stripperdancerbarmaid* at the local gentlemen's club.

Add to all this, Rudolfo. Swimmer gut that ripples under his shirt. Has two jobs. One at the butcher where Twin One buys her chops. At night he tends bar with Twin Two.

You can guess what happens, and how it all plays out like cheap pulp. Black stockings and deception times two.

You can guess how it all ends up with Twin One's husband whacking Rudolfo's open throat with a cinderblock axe.

You can guess how both twins show up at the funeral. Both of them orphaned now of love and lust and even each other.

And never once do they look back to their girlhood. That moment when they stood side by side, dressed identical by their mother. Not even a thought of that birthday they shared a cake and stood on tiptoes together to blow out the candles, their wishes splitting apart in the air just above.

When he Left

It was summer. It was soft exhale of sky and cloudfloat. It was a lemonade glass you rolled on your throat and humid drops of where did he go? Where did he go? It was you should have not stayed in the sun so long, you know how easy you burn. It was a walk on the beach, the sudden screech of gulls like thoughts hanging in the air. It was when he told you he wasn't sure and you told him, it's okay, I'll give you time, but time isn't yours to give. It was strange perfume scent and no way not to smell it. It was telling yourself he fell in a patch of wildflowers. Meanwhile your hair was feathered, your skin drying down to wilt. You, the part of the peach leftover after the succulent flesh is bitten and stripped. The sky a collection of hearts and orange and spill of leftover love.

When he left

It was autumn. It was crunch and pumpkin and all the tricks your heart always makes. Eyescoop and goo and that's what makes a face. And you know it's only pumpkins that work that way because there were no smiles on his face anymore. He wasn't lit from within anymore, and you could feel the breeze each time he walked in the room. You tried to remind him of apple picking and cinnamon and the sweet stickiness of toffee. You were trying to think of what could hold him, what could keep him, and you knew there was nothing but winter coming up soon.

When he left

It was winter. It was raw claw of icy branch where the sun didn't look anymore. It was oh you should have worn a hat which was another way to say you shouldn't have introduced him to your *sisterbestfriendcoworker*. You know how that is just another hole in the ice, another slip and skid and there you are, your car spinning like the hands of time which don't stop, don't stop and you were cleaning the snow slop off the hallway floor, the wood all buckled and warped and rather than go after him one more goddam time, you get on your knees, which are buckled now and warped themselves, what with time taking all it can, stuffing it in a sack, and there you are rubbing circles on the floor that will never feel his footsteps again, your back that will never feel his strum.

When he left

There was no spring.

This is the Part

Where I believe that it was the goddam fault of the night willow, that if it hadn't been so blacked out like it was, bowed so brushy and low, you could have seen your way around it. Could have driven a clean road home like you do every night, except this one.

This is the part where I say it's okay, it's okay. That everyone blows themselves up now and then. You were driving at night, your eyes like cat diamonds, only even then you didn't see how the tree branches seemed to dip out of nowhere, almost as if the sky let go and you were glided like an alligator oozing into a swamp. No one around to hear you calling for help.

This is not the part where you finally say okay, you fell in love with someone else and that's where you were all night.

This is still the part where I shake my head at how fleeting everything is. How lucky you are because anything can happen. How someone can be right there in front of another someone and you blink and one of you is suddenly gone.

Later will be the part where I tell you I'm good, I'm good. You go ahead and take the silver. The children you make with your new love will need to eat with authenticity. You will bring them up to spot a fake. You will bring them up to avoid bad lovers who tell them that they didn't come home that night because they drove into a willow tree, or the willow tree drove into them, or they had no control of the whole situation, and that falling in love with someone else can happen even when you are in love with someone already and you were oozed like an alligator into a swamp or quicksand with no way to stop it. How you wouldn't believe it if you hadn't seen it with your own goddam eyes.

Balance

My father was 20 feet tall. So, there's that.

My mother built him a special house in the backyard. She had to cut away all the trees

Life is balance, she would say. Good days, bad days, it's still your life. Don't scrunch up your nose at not one part of it.

My father would stick his huge hand, the size of a couch cushion, through the window at mealtime, and my mother would load it up with plates of bacon or hot dogs or chops. He'd blow her a kiss and take the food back to his house in our treeless yard.

The hardest part, my mother said, was that this was the only time she saw him anymore. He didn't fit in our house and her going to my father's house in the backyard only reminded her of her favorite trees.

Soon, the other women showed up, lines of them. All of them having heard about my twenty-foot father. All of them curious about, well, you know.

My mother didn't worry. She would sit in a rocking chair on the front porch. She would sit there except for meal time when my father would show up again. She would sit there and rock back and forth in the balance of love, then not love, then love.

That Time the Planet Exploded

Leaving shards of mountain in your soup. The planet exploded, but still enough land, still enough air, and nothing but soup to live on.

Today, like always, you spoon the mountain aside – but what's that shining from the bottom of the can? A key? An actual key? You say this out loud to your husband who isn't there anymore.

A key seems rather useless now that there aren't any doors.

The planet exploded from the inside, not by Man which is what you would have thought. Instead, it was roil and boil and magma. It was oceans clapping shut like mouths. At first, you were glued to the TV, and then, like that, the TV was gone.

You found soup in the leftover supermarket store, the one with the shelves all this way and that like broken teeth. You and the few others armloaded up with cans of soup. You and the few others walking right out with no one to stop you.

You all agreed to spread out because of all the luxurious room you had always dreamed of. You all agreed to start your own countries.

Now, you open your nightly can of soup. You bang it open with a rock because the can opener got swallowed in a lava rush. You have grown used to bits of everything showing up in the can, but a key? You wonder if this was the last act of the soupmaker who was hoping to be remembered, if not saved. You hate these pieces of your used-to-be-world and how it only reminds you that alone is not the luxury you thought it would be.

Some nights you want so badly to look at another face. You even pretend-plan a trip to another one of the countries the few others made. But you remember the agreement. No visits. Danger of new population.

You all decided that the last time you were together, all of your arms hefted with soup cans outside the leftover supermarket store. Goodbye, good luck, flab of another hand on yours for the very last time.

You remember this some days. Forget it on others. Like today, when you eat your soup and this key pops up, and you will stare at this key for hours. You will think about the times you came home from work, your husband on the other side of a lockclick. You will even hold the key in your hands for awhile, press it against the fleshy part of your palm which needs so badly to be touched. Finally, you will hold the key up to your heart. Wonder if there is anything left there to turn.

Father Nails the Doors and Windows Shut

He says we are better off inside. Outside, he says, is made of sickness and guns and inside, we will do just fine.

The living room lamp becomes our sun. We spread towels across the carpet and try to get a tan. At night, when the outside sun is going down, clamping shut the day, Father says we can make up our own minds now about when day is over, and isn't that nice?

Father arranges the kitchen chairs to look like the car in the driveway. He pretend-drives us to school on his way to the job he doesn't go to anymore. He says this way we can make up our own minds about what we want to learn and he doesn't have to face his stupid mule of a boss and isn't that nice?

One day, about two weeks in, Mother poses a question. What about money? What about food? She offers to get herself a waitress job, but Father won't hear of it. Instead, he nails her in the closet, just to be sure.

My little brother starts to draw pictures of the sun. Not the light bulb sun, but with rays like the one in the outside sky. Father takes the drawing away and tells my little brother there will be no more food for him. My little brother reminds him that we haven't eaten in days.

My older brother punches a hole in the attic, climbs out, and drives our real car away. When Father finds out, he harumphs and says that's one less nose to breathe up our air, and isn't that nice?

I don't think it's nice. Never have, and I've been living on sucking candies leftover from Mother's bridge club. But

I'm not so eager to live in a closet so when Father asks again, I tell him yes, yes, it's all very nice.

Good, he nods, the two of us looking at the living room lamp, agreeing that since the sun is still up, why don't we walk into the kitchen and take ourselves a drive.

Radio Water

Every morning that June, we would watch Ralphie dip into the lake behind our summer house. Ralphie came from nuclear country and told us the lake was radioactive.

Radio water, he called it. He never told us much about where he came from so we didn't know if it was a bomb or what. He would just point to the hairless patch above his right ear. He did say that whatever had happened left him mostly immune to further radiation, and that's why he could swim, untouched, in the lake. My little brother told us he didn't believe Ralphie. Said he saw him through the window one day with a razor and shaving cream.

XXX

Father had told us that this would be our final summer at the lake. He said he would be leaving us for good to live with the other family he made when my mother wasn't watching him every goddam minute, which was how my mother would later describe it. My parents didn't speak to each other anymore. She wouldn't even look in his direction. Not when he burned hamburgers on the grill or when he zoomed his car away each night after supper.

XXX

One morning, late in July, we were watching Ralphie like always. How he would dip his toe in, then up to his waist, finally knifing himself through the water to the other side where the rowboats knocked and swayed. Ralphie explained that the rowboats were also immune and that's why the water hadn't eaten them.

XXX

One other morning, my father showed us photos of his other family. All of us looking, except, of course, for my mother. Same number of kids in his other family. Two boys. Two girls. They were younger than us. Newer. They were swimming in a lake. They were eating perfect hamburgers.

XXX

Later, we went outside to see Ralphie coming out of the radio water and wrapping himself in a *Spiderman* towel. He looked at us watching him and held up his right hand. Two fingers only. "Guess I'm not completely immune," he called over. Beads of radio water on his face and my little brother telling us that Ralphie was folding his other fingers back. Ralphie palmed the water off his face and walked over to my brother. "Listen, pipsqueak," he said, his chest glistening in the sunlight, glowing almost uranium, "I'd throw you in, but that water would fizz you up alive."

XXX

The next time my father showed us his new family, my little brother wandered outside, slapped the screen door closed behind him and walked over to the water's edge. He just stood there looking at the spot where the boats sway.

XXX

I walked outside one night after supper. My father was sitting by the hammock that was always filled with mosquitoes from the rain. By this time, every other night, my father had driven off to his other family. But not that night. That night, he was sitting very still. Hands in his lap and looking down at the ground. We all went to bed and it wasn't till later when something woke me. I looked out the window to see my father loading up the car with all of his suitcases, along with a bundle of some kind, the exact shape of my little brother.

XXX

Ralphie told everyone the next day that my little brother must have wandered into the radio water and just fizzed away. "Like my fingers," he said holding up his hand, "like my hair." I thought back to my little brother doubting everything Ralphie said. I thought back to last night watching my brother disappearing into my father's other family.

XXX

Now that my mother didn't have my father to ignore, she became chatty and younger somehow. We never talked about my little brother anymore. Ralphie's story seemed to be enough for her. It's like my brother fizzing away in the radio water was an easier thing to believe.

XXX

End of August and my mother told us we would be coming back next summer. She had fallen in love with the nearby hiking trails and woke us up at 6 a.m. each morning for a run. She ignored the men who came to examine the lake, who told her the water was safe to swim in. Ignored Ralphie even when his hair grew in and she could see his fingers plain as day. Ignored the photo my father sent with my little brother seated on his knee, and smiling as if for the first time in his life. My mother waved it away and said that's a boy who looks like your brother. That doesn't make him your brother. When she said it, she looked off across the lake at the boats still swaying and knocking. The boats that maybe even only looked like boats.

Then, Thenner, Thennest

Then

He gets born somehow. Never even knew his mother. If he did know his mother, he would wish he didn't. Lots of late-night poker games and booze as her belly swelled into a watermelon. Lost the unborn pup to *four-of-a-kind*. I'm sorry *four-of-a-kind* said, but my wife wants a baby so bad. Worked out for everyone except the pup who grows into a boy and finds out about God when the *four-of-a-kind's* wife comes down with pneumonia and *four-of-a-kind* catches it and they both die leaving the boy five years old and alone. The boy says, God, what the hell? God tells him go to your room.

Thenner

He gets married somehow. His wife is away all the time, so he barely knows her. Pops out a couple of pups so he figures they must have spent a few nights together. The pups grow into horrible boys. Yes, all children are wonderful, but these really aren't. Hold him up for his paycheck each week so they can go play poker and knock up strange women. Knock up is a harsh term to be sure, but these are harsh boys. They carve their initials into one another's backs for practice. Then they turn to him and say, "Pop, you're next." When he complains to his wife who happens to walk in at that very moment so she can get dressed up to see her lover, she laughs and says "oh relax, they are having fun." Then she puts on her fire red shoes and shakes off her underwear. God, he says, what the hell? God tells him go live in your car.

Thennest

He gets old somehow. Slope-chested and claw-fingered. There are days he swears he never knew anyone, never did anything. A girl shows up at his nursing home. I think you're my grandpa, she says. He remembers the horrible boys, the horrible wife and says are you going to cut me? By this time, the vanilla pudding is hardened in its plastic cup on the tray. Every so often a bell from the hall. The girl is young, teenager maybe. Blond hair like his was once, blue eyes like his wife's. I love you, the girl finally says. You're my family. He says, God, what the hell? You wait my entire lifetime to give me this scrap of happiness? Here, God heaves a God-sigh, rattling trees for miles around, tells him live, just go live, just go live.

Is it Cold Where You Are?

After all this time, my father shows up. Only thing is, he's dead.

"Good to see you," I tell him.

"Don't get smart," he says. So, it's like that.

We both know it's not good to see him.

That's because he was always broke, gambling or something like that, and he'd yell at my mother all the time. A couple of snarly dogs, they were. And then him selling my stereo when I was in school and calling me a baby for being upset. *It was for the family*, he insisted. *Put those tears back in your head.*

Now he shows up, all ghost and out of excuses.

"Why are you here?" I ask. "I don't have a stereo for you to steal." He's grayer, more prune than I remember. He looks old. He looks dead. Dead is older than old.

"You should forget about that." He sits down. He doesn't even need a chair.

"Tell me," he says. "Is it cold where you are?"

"You mean here?" I say. "You mean five feet away from you?"

"I'm not really here," he says. "It only seems that way."

I was always making that mistake. Like the time I was little and I sat on his lap. He was a cradle. A home. *Who's my best little girl?* he said. I said *me? Is it me?* He booped my nose. He was right. there.

"It's warm here," I tell him. "It's the temperature of your hand when someone has squeezed it and the heat of it is still on yours."

"I have to go now," he says. That's the father I know. Always one foot into tomorrow and me never invited. "It's burning where I am," he says. I think yeah, I think about the devil licks toasting his feet.

And then, just as he disappears for forever, I hope, I remember the other nights like that one. Me, a shiver in my bedroom. My parents downstairs. Thud of furniture, breaking of plates and me turning up the volume to full blast on the stereo, that one album, *The Who*, the one I played so often, even when the needle skipped and played that one part over and over and over.

Middle of Night

Too late for candy or games. Scratch of Mommy's slippers in the hall. We are three days without my father who left to who knows where? Came home from work like a night of storms and slammed his fist on the table. Saying words like "fired" and "bastard." Angry, like when he told Mommy he never wanted kids, and me, listening at the door. A terrible thing to never want your father back, but I'm thinking of tomorrow morning, breakfast of oranges, bacon curling into smiles, Mommy all to myself, and the cloud of my father in someone else's sky.

Bad Fish

Brad and Bella, newly newly, having to spend their Miami honeymoon in a broken hotel and Bella sick from last night's fish. Who orders room service in a dump like this, but still they were hungry, tired, and Brad insisting on romance.

Just past dawn, the sun a peek in the sky and still it streaks in through the flimsy curtains, onto the cakey walls with the green velvet stencil of palm trees, waving, waving, always waving. Brad stands over the bed as Bella moans and clutches the pillow. "It's all that waving making me sick," she manages to say. To which Brad answers, "Ha, I thought you said it was the fish."

Brad is head of household now and wants to fix the world, so he takes the writhing Bella, herself a squirmy fish, and throws her in a pounding shower. The water is surprisingly certain for such a broken-down dump and the steam is rising around her. "I can't fix this if you won't tell me the truth," he says.

Bella, under the crush of water, punches Brad in the gut and screams "I only married you because I couldn't have your brother." Brad flashes back to his brother, a slippery fish, himself, always inviting Bella to the beach and them not-so-secretly winking at each other.

Bella is heaving now and says, it wasn't the fish that made me sick, it wasn't the wavy walls. It was kissing you last night. Brad grabs Bella by the face, pinches her lips into a fish mouth and lets the crush of water stream in as if to flush the words right out of her.

Brad is stunned and shuts off the water, feels a jolt of panic when Bella crumples to the bottom of the shower stall. His stomach is sore from where Bella punched him and starts to churn. Maybe the fish is catching up with him, too. But more likely from the murder he has just committed and what Bella said about his brother. If only she hadn't told him that. Still, he realizes he insisted on it, said that truth was the only way to fix things. He walks back inside picks up the bedside phone, an ancient rotary and dials the police, his hands still slick. The phone slips from his hands, the tinny voice saying *911 – what's your emergency?*

From outside the Miami morning drifts in, sun and coconut breeze and Brad feeling proud of how he fixed everything, just like he wanted. But then it hits him that the police will un-fix everything – questions and headlines and everything about Brad's brother. The truth doesn't fix anything if it breaks up the rest of your life.

No, instead he will let the chambermaid find Bella, swollen and bloated, let her assume she died from the force of the shower, or maybe the bad fish, after all. Happy now, Brad puts on his shoes and grabs his suitcase, heads off to catch the next plane to Cuba, or Fiji, or France or anywhere that he won't hear the tinny voice coming from the phone on the floor – *hello, hello is anybody there?*

This is a Secret, So Shhhhh

Bennett doesn't know that I'm leaving.

Bennett is a hill all swaddled in Grandma Holler's quilt. Patches of gingham and dots. Wedding present she made with her twisty fingers and tiny sight. Family treasure until Bennett drunk-ruined it one too many times. Now, it's his all alone.

I ease our honeymoon suitcase from the closet. Hawaii stickers, Hula dancer waving hello. It opens like a chattery mouth. Like next door Ruth who will surely swoop in on Bennett, like I know she has before.

Like the times I came home early and found wiped-off lipstick on a wine glass, Grandma Holler's quilt in a forgotten, nauseous heap.

Bennett goes from gurgle to snore to gurgle. I throw one blouse into the suitcase. I'm going to need lots of room. I flip the floorboard where I've hidden the money. The 40K Grandma Holler had wrapped in the quilt. That I hid so good that Bennett has torn up the apartment a time or two and still never found it.

The night we opened the quilt and the money fell out and we covered it, joked it was my lover and I was still stupid and in love. I have to keep my lover hid, I told him with a wink.

The money goes quiet into the suitcase. Bennett will look for it way before he looks for me. I look at Bennett under the quilt. Pile of bad money, Grandma Holler would say.

I close up the suitcase's open blabbery mouth. Without another sound, we slip secret out the door and into the world.

Later

They wake up to the neighborhood on fire. Their bedroom wall is a face of windows. The wife thought that all that glass would be cheery. This was back when cheery was an option, a word she could say without feeling ironic.

Later, it will come out that the fire started in Stone's garage. Too many gasoline cans and so on.

Later, later, it will come out that the wife was in love with Stone, and that was the reason she ran in the direction of his house rather than out of town like everyone else.

But for now, the husband and wife are running around scooping up contact lenses, the go-to bag she prepared for events just like this, small cans of tuna. All the time, the smoke alarms screaming.

Just as they get to the front door, the wife stops. "I forgot something," she says. Later, she will confess to the jury that the diary, this thing she forgot, the only thing that ironically survived the fire, was in fact filled with plans to explode her house with the gasoline Stone was holding.

"No time," the husband says and scoops her over the threshold, outside and opposite of the marriage way.

Once outside, the wife wriggles free. She disappears into a narrow carve in the fire that closes up after her. The husband calls her name before himself going up in flame.

Later, later, later she will sit in her tiny jail cell. No one's wife anymore and the wall a face of stone. *Stone, stone, stone*, she will say every morning when she wakes for the rest of her life. She will never even see the irony of this.

Last Swim

Late August, and one dying half hour till the rooftop pool closes up for the season. The end of summer sky is holding a fistful of rain.

50-year-old Mabel, her fleshy arm like a slab of cod fillet as she hangs on the edge of the pool. The water prisms her wearing a two-piece she doesn't have the figure for anymore. Her eyes are fixed on Marty, also 50, who is doing his 20 laps.

The lifeguard, high school senior this year and glad that soon he won't have to yell at old people anymore. His uncle, the building manager, told him that since no one ever drowns there, this would be the main part of the job.

Mabel lets go of the edge and paddles into the center until Marty laps by. "I want to talk," she says.

He doesn't even stop. Splashes and cuts the water like a boat motor.

"I love you," Mabel calls after him. "I love you."

The lifeguard is tweeting his whistle. He doesn't really have to with only those two in the pool. "Five minutes," he holds up the fingers on his left hand.

"Oh honey," Mable turns to the lifeguard. "Don't you have some cute little girlfriend you could call?"

The lifeguard thinks about Susie, the other lifeguard who left for college last week. With her red danger lipstick and belly button ring. Maybe that's who Mabel means.

The summer sky is getting darker, heavier almost. Any other night there would be thunder.

Marty stops his laps right next to Mabel. "Listen," he says, water beading on his brow, his dark hair in strands. "I don't love you. My wife was away. I was lonely."

The lifeguard can hear their voices. Hears what they are saying and doesn't want to.

"No *you* listen," Mabel says, "I could stop by your apartment. Have a nice little chat with your wife."

The lifeguard has been trained to watch for trouble brewing in the pool. Well, not trained, exactly. Warned by his uncle. His uncle also warned him that Susie put in a complaint, said she was there to earn money for college, not be groped by some twerpy little high school senior.

"You wouldn't do that. My wife is sick. You might even kill her," Marty says and goes back to his laps.

The lifeguard tweets his whistle. "Two minutes."

"That would actually solve the problem," Mabel says as Marty swims by her again. With that, she swims towards the steps leading out of the pool.

"No wait," Marty catches up to her, her foot on the first step. "I do love you. I do." He wipes the water out of his eyes. "Chlorine," he says. "Messes with my brain."

"Well," Mabel says, "if you love me, then you'll be glad if I tell your wife."

Marty dives under the water and pulls her by the ankle back into the pool. Mabel struggles to get away. They are flipping and flapping, spraying water everywhere. The lifeguard thinks how much these two look like the fish his uncle catches when they go out on his boat on Sundays.

"Time!" the lifeguard yells. Then he tweets his whistle ten times.

Mabel and Marty continue thrashing around in the water. Mabel calling out help me! help me! The lifeguard stands there, thinking not about them, but about how he should call Susie up at college and ask for another chance.

He tweets again and finally gives up and begins to drain the pool. The water lowering, the two of them rising into the naked air, a drop of late summer rain about to fall out of the sky.

Why You Can't Believe the Weather Report, No Way, No How

It's still yesterday somewhere, almost tomorrow somewhere else. One minute, you're getting a fistful of sunshine slamming you in the face, next minute, it's softened to butter. Time zones are the problem, everything different everywhere else and I'm trying to explain this to Charley, who is always walking towards New Zealand, where it's tomorrow and he'd be younger than everyone else. I tell him now is always now, that time isn't a butterfly and he just nods and turns on the Weather Channel. Watching for tornadoes in faraway places. Charley is enough of a tornado for me, scooping me up in his lovearms and slamming me down to the ground. Sometimes I wake up next day, I am wreckage, I am bonetwist, and look over there by the side of the road, my heart a pulsing pocketbook filled with how I could have hid from him in a bathtub, how one minute he is sunshine at five o'clock and next minute he's midnight and I can have all the go-bags I want, I can pack medicine and extra clothes and be ready to run at a moment's notice, but I look out the window, nothing but a stitch of cloud, and I can't tell how bad it will get, because when I look into Charley's eyes, nothing but soft blue hope, and there's no possible way I could have known.

This Won't Take Long, Will It?

When it's autumn and it's leafcurl and twigsnap and our old next-door neighbor is raking and raking and we want to help him because he is, himself, a crackled tree. When it's autumn and the mounds of leaves are piling all around our next-door neighbor and he waves in our direction. *Hey kids!* he even says. And before we can wave back at him, our father is calling us into the garage.

When it's autumn and it's cider tang and pumpkin squish, and our father is our father, but didn't he see our neighbor? See the barky scratch and wrinkles that have written the story of his life all over his face? We walk inside the garage, all benches and tools and paint, and our father is fixing a lawn chair. Reweaving a hole in the seat. Frayed green and white plastic fabric, and we don't know why this is important, now when it's autumn. Our father points us all to a bench so we can watch what he is doing. So we will know for ourselves someday. One of us finally says, *this won't take long, will it?* Our father stops weaving and says well, that isn't the point.

One of us wants to know what *is* the point, but we all know not to ask. Once, when it was summer, lemonade squinch and skeeterbuzz, some of us squeezing into the lawn chair, we asked why our mother went away. How we didn't know if she had died or if it was something else. We wanted to know the point of her absence and our father wouldn't talk to us for a week until one of us finally said, well now it's like we have no parents.

When it's later autumn, turkeysniff and firecrack, and we haven't seen our neighbor in a month, we wonder why he went away. The leaves have been falling and falling and one of us even says that the old man is buried underneath. Another one says that they heard that the old man fell over, timber, from a heart attack. That it didn't take long and that death probably waved at him from across the yard. When our father hears this, he says that's not any truer than what happened to our mother and that the less we think about death, the better, that life is only here for a minute or so and it really doesn't take long. We wonder if this is the point he is trying to make, the hang of snow, heavy, invisible. The winter about to begin.

An Hour Past my Bedtime

Me and Shady Granger playing grownup. Me and he. Just past 12 years old. Me chugging an empty whiskey bottle and him fake-smoking a cigarette. Pretending we are like our own parents. His family came from over there. Forbidden part of town. Part of town where the poor folks live, my daddy always said, and it's best we don't go trying to mix it up. I loved Shady's careful smile that opened like the moon.

Saturday mornings, my mama sleeping it off on the couch and Daddy at his office like always, and I'd call Shady, quick come over. Sometimes, Shady was busy watching the little kids, with his own Mama scrubbing a rich lady's floor, his daddy circling the paper looking for work. Other days, Shady would ride his bike over and we'd head back to the porch, smoking and drinking and laughing. The afternoon drifting into a sweet, slow evening and him sneaking off before my daddy got home and my mama got up. My daddy would ask me over dinner why I was looking so damn happy. I couldn't wind down. An hour past my bedtime and I could hear Shady's voice calling me from way across town.

Ten Years Past My Bedtime

Me and Shady Granger, grownups now. Me and he. Ran off together middle of the night. My daddy looked and looked. Finally gave up, heart attack, I heard somewhere. My mama never got over the sting of his death and me leaving.

Somewhere in all this, Shady stopped smiling at me. It's like he took away the moon. I went shrill and started drinking for real. Shady blamed me for losing his own family and would huff himself out of the house. Gone for days at a time. I'd look out the window, the sky going aquamarine, like my mama used to say. Didn't know why she didn't call it blue. Thought maybe it was a made-up drunk word. Who knows? Maybe it was.

Thirty Years Past My Bedtime

Me and Shady Granger with our own grownup kids. Me and he all over again. I watched our girl, Sarah, some nights looking at the moon for answers to love. I watched our boy Griff squeal the Volkswagen out of the driveway. He would be all slicked up and flowered and on his way to break a heart. Me, I became just like my mama. The bottle full, then empty, then full. Shady running out back on the porch, his cigarette smoke curling up around the moon.

A Lifetime Past My Bedtime

Me, but no Shady Granger. Me without he. Shady got a fever that burned him up from the inside. Kids don't call much anymore like they promised. Some nights now, the house is so alone and cold I can hear teardrops from the moon.

My mama always used to say that life is a singer of sad, sad, songs. They are a hum in your ear as you go along chasing happiness, chasing love. And it's only at the end of things, when you finally stop, you start to make out the melody, the words become sharp and clear, too late, really, for them to help at all, the bittersweet strain of them smoking up into the air.

The Switch

One day, the sun goes out. *Pfft,* like a light bulb. And then the light bulbs, too. Suddenly, noon is midnight black. Stars come out, but they don't help.

Bloom, as usual, barely notices. Draped like always, like a raggy old blanket in his easy chair.

Mrs. Bloom is now a voice in the dark. She moves towards Bloom. "You should have bought candles like I told you," she says, her voice like a potato peeler.

"Don't you care, the sun went out? And right when I'm making your lunch," she continues. "I can't make tuna salad in the dark."

Bloom shifts deeper into his chair. "It's okay," he says. "They'll turn the switch back on. Just be patient."

"What about ham?" Mrs. Bloom says. "I got it on special."

"You know ham keeps me awake."

"Mr. Picky," Mrs. Bloom says. "And enough already with the switch nonsense. This is what you said when the river stopped, or when we went to the beach that time and the waves went dead."

"They got switches for all of it. All of it," Bloom says. "They got switches in North Carolina."

"I'm making you a ham sandwich and you'll eat it."

Her voice sweltering the apartment like a heat wave, like the time the cold weather switched off, *boom,* just like that.

Bloom's stomach rumbling now and it doesn't matter how loud, he can still hear Mrs. Bloom's voice.

And Bloom doesn't know why he didn't think of it before, but he slugs himself up out of his chair and finds his way to the room they only use now for old magazines. Way in the back, a tiny closet, the switch for Mrs. Bloom.

He can still hear her nattering like a rainstorm, and then with a simple flick, it stops. *She* stops.

Bloom finds his way back to the chair. Contentment filling him, even his stomach. Quiet now, Mrs. Bloom frozen in place in the kitchen. Tuna waiting to be mixed in the bowl when he turns her back on, later, when the sun switches back on. Her mouth open till then wide and empty like a forgotten cave.

Boat Sink

Eleven knew that it was a bad night for boating, but Twelve had insisted. So much of their marriage had been like this. Eleven said one thing, Twelve said another. This time, Twelve got his way by saying he wanted to look at Eleven's hair in the moonlight, how it rippled and flowed, how the shine of it echoed the stripe of light on the water. Eleven finally gave up and went along. Besides, she reasoned, it was the least she could do now that she was going to leave him.

Twelve had other woman. Schools of them, it seemed. He couldn't help it, he would tell her, not his fault. They flipped and flapped themselves at him and what on earth was he to do?

She told him how ridiculous that sounded and they would be better off apart. That's when he begged her to take this one last ride, to the spot on the lake where he had proposed.

It was 9 p.m. Long after the boathouse had closed and Twelve said, it's okay, we'll be safe with the moon. He freed up a rickety rowboat, boards loose and splintered. They rowed themselves out to the center where Twelve pulled a bottle of wine out of his knapsack. Eleven was charmed in an ancient way.

That's when the fish, huge, and flecked silver in the white light, punched itself up through the boatfloor.

Eleven had never seen a fish that strong, a fish that stupid, one that would literally fish itself into a boat, to flip and flap itself right there and lay itself down as prey.

Only one thing to do now, Eleven thought, and hooked her foot over the side of the boat, which had begun lowering itself, inch by inch. Rather than go with her, Twelve grabbed the fish, which was still alive, and said, "I can use this to stop up the hole."

"No wait," Eleven said, "you leave that poor girl alone!" She has no idea where this was coming from. This empathy, this understanding of how desperate this fish must have been. Maybe the fish just needed companionship. Maybe the nearness of a man. Eleven started to wonder if she should believe what Twelve had been saying about his other woman and she felt an almost forgiveness for him.

But by then Twelve was little more than a blubber of bubbles. The fish, set free, was skimming away under the waterskin. Eleven had no choice but to swim alone towards shore, the boat sinking behind her as she swam into a white stripe of moon, her hair flowing and rippling out around her.

Ricky Watson Doesn't Love Me, for a Change

But that's not new. My best friend, Mo, says nothing's new, not the burn-up sun, or the wind-swish trees. Everything's been the same since it all banged apart. Mo's the only one who sees any good at all in Ricky Watson, and she will tell me for a full five minutes. Mo can't say anything that isn't an essay, (it's why she does so good in English class.) Ms. Tyler will even say, "oh c'mon, Maureen, give someone else a chance." Mo doesn't see the point of that – if a thing is right, it's right, is all. So, it's no surprise that when I begin to cry about Ricky Watson and how completely gone he is, Mo finishes her speech about him, looks at me square and says, "well, let's go get him back."

I tell Mo she's crazy, which is not a thing that will stick – Mo likes being crazy, thinks it's kind of exotic. My mom pops in, big *Aquanet* do, and asks, "what would you two lovelies like for supper?" Mo's pop is out of work again, and she can eat here all she wants, is what Mom has been known to say. Mo just answers, "whatever's good, Mrs. June." I'm June, by the way, so you know.

Mo says that whatever we have for supper, we can pretend it's something else. We can put on a couple of berets and pretend we are in Paris like the Van Gogh painting we saw in art class. I am thinking we are too old for this kind of pretending but don't say so what with Mo's pop being out of work and how that's really enough of a thing.

I've also been thinking that Mo wants me back with Ricky Watson more than *I* want me back with Ricky Watson. After the way he comes and goes, I'm tempted to tell her to forget it. Mom serves us casserole for supper which I personally hate because it's nothing but a lot of foods pushed together rather then one whole thing like a hamburger you can depend on. Mom says casserole is a good way to stretch a food dollar. Mo scarfs it down and says it was "magnifique, Mrs. June."

After supper, we go to my room to write Ricky Watson a letter. Mo says everyone texts and DMs and how delicious would it be for Ricky Watson to find this in his mailbox. We can even scent it with Mom's *eau de cologne*, she says. I say okay, and even let Mo write the letter because she's so good with essays and all.

Later that week, when Ricky Watson calls just like Mo said he would, I am not as happy as you might think. Mom calls me aside "without Maureen," she says. Once alone she says maybe it wasn't such a good idea to let Maureen write that letter to Ricky Watson. I'm thinking it's just because Mom doesn't like Ricky Watson much, but to my surprise it's not that at all.

"As you get older, June, you are going to want to do more on your own." She says if I had let things be with Ricky Watson, he probably would have come back his ownself, but now I can never be sure. And I'm thinking that maybe Mom is right.

That night at supper, I tell Mo I'm not gonna be around too much this week because I'm back with Ricky Watson now. Mom nods her approval behind Mo who looks deep into her casserole plate. Mom assures Mo that she can eat here as much as she wants, June or no. Mo sits up and says oh, that's okay and by the way, she forgot to tell us but her pop got another job.

"Well," Mom says, "I'm glad to hear about your father, but you are welcome anytime." I tell her yes, that's right, because after all, she's family now. The word family is like a piece of random hot dog or tuna or whatever Mom put in the casserole. I taste it but it washes down my throat kind of quick. I tell Mo that in her honor we can have our dessert in Paris. "If you like," I tell her, "we can even wear our berets."

Perfect

In the low-light of morning, Mildred eases, teardrop, out of bed. She hasn't been much for sleeping, but last night was different, what with Harry visiting in a dream.

Everyone warned her. How death perfects a person. Her mother, pinching her arm at the funeral. "Look around," her mother whispered. "How many of his women are here?"

Mildred had known, of course. How could she not, what with Harry's constant preening and spice cologne. Mildred knew, but was love-prisoned, the bars of it metal and strong.

Egg yolk skittering now in the breakfast pan and Mildred can't forget the dream. What with Harry telling her to meet him by the river. On the high rock ledge where they had that first summersweet picnic. The jab and snag of the rocks and the two of them going naked and in love.

In the dream, Harry tells her his death is lonely. What with her still alive, able to eat and sleep and breathe.

She had thought of this herself, of course. What with day and day and day blinking its stupid pain at her. She had thought of wristslit and pillswallow, but there was something always stopping her, what with fear kicking in, one last hope kicking in.

In the dream, Harry is perfect. His other women hidden from his face. His tongue gone empty of lies. And the dream itself, what with its broken nature, turning Harry to a bird to a river to a rock.

Mildred finishes her breakfast. It would be easy to go to the river, she thinks. Take the cobbled path up to the ledge. Fall teardrop into the river.

But, by now, the sun is full. Late morning when the truth scorches itself into her eyes. Harry will never be better than he was last night in the dream. Will never love her more than that.

Later that night, when Mildred goes to bed, she knows that Harry will be waiting there for her, longing for her, wanting her, and so she slips perfect into sleep.

Snout Face

Not now, but soon, I will be leaving Busby. Busby, whose eyes are dark marbles, whose eyes don't meet mine anymore. His face is long, like a bear face, his mouth wide and gaping like he could swallow a salmon whole. Soon it will be the barren season, dry and famine, like a town up north where starving polar bears invade, just clomping down Main Street, nosing into garbage cans, and the people adjust by leaving their car doors open for pedestrians to dive into. No one blames a bear for being a bear, and so I can't blame Busby for being Busby. I knew he was snort and prowl when I met him. Now, I leave my heart open so he can dive in anytime. Like when he's lost another job because his boss was a dick or some other Busby logic. But soon, not now, not today, I will get tired of it all. Get tired of being flipped and flapped in Busby's snout mouth. I will restart myself in forage mode, adapt myself for a long, hungry winter, curl up in the hand of my own empty heart.

Milk

My mother and the milkman, because she is very old, and they used to leave milk in glass bottles in metal boxes and somehow it never went bad. Tuesdays, my mother would lean in the doorway, all sashay and catpurr while my father rattled to work on the 8:15. And my mother and the milkman, later rattling in my brother's room, and my brother in the Vietnam sun, his shaky grenade hand at the top of his arm. How later, months or even a year went by, before we got the telegram. Mother shaking in the loop of Daddy's arms. Milk sold now in cartons. In the supermarket. Where anyone could watch.

Not Again

Farmer Joe says this to the empty air. Eggshells everywhere and the dirt floor of the barn slick with goo that has oozed out of the broken shells. Chickens scattered around, most dead, others on their way. A tortured cluck and then another, slow and slower like an old-fashioned watch running out.

This could be anything, Farmer Joe thinks. He stands in the doorframe like a useless scarecrow. Maybe it was bird murder by the kids from down the way. Maybe it was raccoons. He thinks back to last Halloween and the broken pumpkins on the front doorstep. The chunks of ribs and the orange pulp that never quite washed off the concrete. It would have all seemed like an innocent prank if it hadn't been the same day his Sarah died.

It is nearly 5 p.m. Sun lower now in the late autumn sky and chill coming up. How did he miss the commotion, bird squawk, and fence rattle? Problem of working the farm all alone. You just can't blame yourself, he thinks. Same thing he told Sarah the night she lost the baby. Him, touching her moistened forehead as she cried and cried, said they shoulda called Doc Taylor, that the midwife was just a slip of a thing.

Six months later, Sarah gone, too. Broken heart, it was.

So now, he is looking at Halloween. First whole year since Sarah's gone, and here are these dead chickens, broken eggs. All of it filling up the air like burning leaves. Farmer Joe squaring himself, he picks up the broom and starts sweeping the shells. Then, he shovels the chickens into a pile, and hoses down the dirt floor. The last of the day's sun comes in the door behind him. Like angel light, like Sarah tapping on his shoulder. It makes him think how memory is an egg. How you can hold it and heft it in your palm. He kneels down on the floor, Picks up a tousle of rags and starts to scrub the stain that, if he lets it, will soak itself in.

Same Old, Same Old

Riley says it's five o'clock somewhere and that's all I need to hear because that means he's off on a tooty-toot-toot and that can happen any day at whatever o'clock but does it have to be an hour before my parents get here and last night's dishes still a crusty mountain in the sink and no I'm not doing them because damn it's Riley's turn even though I know he isn't a my turn kind of guy and I knew that going in but thought that he was different only because the night we first met IRL at Clancy's bar and we moved from our quiet hamburger table in the back to the front where all the regulars were and he kept yelling my turn! my turn! when it was time to buy rounds and he liked all the backslapping love he was getting and what was it in me that thought that was okay and I'm still trying to figure that out with Dr. Joe my secret therapist and how long is that gonna take and if Riley finds out that I'm seeing a therapist behind his back and it's all about him he will freak and move out or maybe just drink up the left side of town and I will have to explain to my parents how I ruined ANOTHER relationship and I don't know if that's any easier than trying to explain why Riley is splayed out across the couch drunken starfish just about an hour from now.

Lovertrees

The forest knows all about them. The forest being the other trees, the scampery bunnies, the rock knots sitting by the gurgly streams. The forest knows about the lovertrees smack in the middle that somehow stay rooted but move towards one another at night.

The whole forest knows, but not the people. The people who wander through each day and scatter home before the lowering sun cuts spatters of light through it all.

An owl shows up, perches itself nearby. Hoots its owly warning as the lovertrees inch towards one another. *They'll cut you both down,* he warns the lovertrees, *or put you together in a museum.*

The lovertrees need each other too much to listen. They whisper comfort. Say things like *we didn't do anything.* Their barks against each other now, their leaves mingled, their branches entwined.

But then, one day, a hiker. Tired and wanting to feel the nightgauze of the forest. He uncurls his bedroll right between the lovertrees before they've had a chance to move. *What a spot,* the hiker says into the air. The lovertrees look at one another. *I could come here every night.* The hiker continues, *maybe even build a tiny house,* The hiker smiles and beds himself down.

Above all this, the stars. Around all this, the forest. All of it watching the lovertrees, separate and still, their pain breathing into the sky.

My Extra Husband

Sleeps each night at the foot of the bed. He doesn't seem to know I see him. He is oil-coiffed and cliff-shouldered. Shadow of every man I ever wanted, never got. My real husband sees him, too. I can tell. Smiles and calls him a beast I built out of wishes. *Look at the limits he puts on your life,* my real husband almost-says. *Your made-up, extra husband travels you everywhere, perfumes the air before you breathe it in. All this pretending makes me tired,* my real husband wants to say, but doesn't. Instead, he pulls up the covers. Turns himself to the wall.

Sister

She'd follow me, puppy that she was, the two of us new in the bicycle wind. The mist of adolescence just ahead but not just yet. She'd grab the flounce of my jacket, she on her roller skates, me on my bike. She'd squeal me to go faster, go faster. I wanted to slow down to an ooze. Never wanted to get to the part where her daughter calls one night to say she's gone. How even now, I can't help but look behind sometimes to see if she's still there.

Acknowledgment is gratefully made to the following journals in which these stories originally appeared:

Night is a Man, *Five South*;

Fishsweat, *Cleaver*;

How to Answer a Door, *Maryland Literary Review*;

In Another Language, Your Name Means Murder, *Monofiction*;

Mimi Comes to the Door, *Psaltery & Lyre*;

Rumble, *Ellipsis Zine*;

Dad Always Looked Like a Mountain, *Bull*;

Dirt, *Journal of Compressed Creative Arts*;

Anywhere by the Sea, *Trampset*;

Cross Country, *Bending Genres*;

The We Part, *Journal of Compressed Creative Arts*;

Lady Macbeth at the Nail Salon, *Gargoyle*;

Mandy Wants to Touch the Horizon, *The Phare*;

This isn't Anything, *Okay Donkey, Best Small Fictions, 2022*;

Remoting, *Ghost Parachute*;

Drunkdaddy, *Cleaver*;

Twins, Prediction, *MOSHLIT*;

When he left, *Pithead Chapel*;

This is the Part, *Mayday*;

Balance, *Gone Lawn*;

That Time the Planet Exploded, *Soft Star*;

Father Nails the Doors and Windows Shut, *Bull*;

Radio Water, *Fictive Dream*; *Flash Fiction America* (Norton Anthology);

Then, Thenner, Thennest, *Fictive Dream*;

Is it Cold Where You Are?, *Roi Fainenant*;

Middle of Night, *Porterhouse Review*;

Bad Fish, *Fictive Dream*;

This is a Secret, so Shhhhh, *Leon Literary Review*;

Later, *Ghost Parachute*;

Last Swim, *Bull*;

Perfect, *MacQueen's Quinterly*;

Snout Face, *Peatsmoke Journal*;

Milk, *Porterhouse Review*;

Not Again, *MacQueen's Quinterly*;

Same Old, Same Old, *Disappointed Housewife*;

Lovertrees, *Ten x Ten*;

My Extra Husband, *Subliminal Journal*;

Sister, *Boston Literary Magazine*.

Francine Witte's poetry and flash fiction have appeared in numerous journals and anthologies. Her latest flash fiction collection is *Just Outside the Tunnel of Love* (Blue Light Press) and her poetry collection *Some Distant Pin of Light* (Cervena Barva Press) is forthcoming in late 2024. She is the flash fiction editor for *South Florida Poetry Journal* and for FLASH BOULEVARD. She lives in NYC. Francinewitte.com

Author photo by Mark Strodl

MORE ROADSIDE PRESS TITLES:

By Plane, Train or Coincidence
Michele McDannold

Prying
Jack Micheline, Charles Bukowski and Catfish McDaris

Wolf Whistles Behind the Dumpster
Dan Provost

Busking Blues: Recollections of a Chicago Street Musician and Squatter
Westley Heine

Unknowable Things
Kerry Trautman

How to Play House
Heather Dorn

Kiss the Heathens
Ryan Quinn Flanagan

St. James Infirmary
Steven Meloan

Street Corner Spirits
Westley Heine

A Room Above a Convenience Store
William Taylor Jr.

Resurrection Song
George Wallace

MORE ROADSIDE PRESS TITLES:

Nothing and Too Much to Talk About
Nancy Patrice Davenport

Bar Guide for the Seriously Deranged
Alan Catlin

Born on Good Friday
Nathan Graziano

Under Normal Conditions
Karl Koweski

Clown Gravy
Misti Rainwater-Lites

Walking Away
Michael D. Grover

All in a Pretty Little Row
Dan Provost

These Are the People in Your Neighbourhood
Jordan Trethewey